This book belongs to:

____

"Look deep into nature, and then you will understand everything better."
~Albert Einstein"

Published and distributed by A & J Publishing, LLC

Illustrations by: Danner James

Photograph of tree:by Ryan McGuire, Gratisography www.gratisography.com

Copyright iStock Photo/2158309 and 19636988

ISBN 978-1-942899-12-9 hardback

Library of Congress Control Number: 2015934607

2015.04.06

This book is dedicated to the students of Charles Pinckney Elementary School in Mount Pleasant, South Carolina, who have discovered and now cherish the gift of reading.

Note to the reader…..

In today's hectic and fast-paced world, we often forget that the overall quality of our lives is to a great extent dependent on the manner in which we treat our natural environment. The forests of the world are playing an ever increasing role in the economic, social, and spiritual quality of life.

If we are to continue to enjoy nature's gifts, we must all share in conserving and nurturing the natural world in which we live.

"Go to the forest to meet the wise green friends."
Mehmet Murat ildan

Nikki and the Tree Keeper

Geoff Collins

Illustrations by
Danner James

Nikki and the Tree Keeper

Nikki Smith was a seventh grader in Miss Farley's class at Mill City Middle School in Mill City, Montana. Nobody paid much attention to him. It wasn't that the other kids in the class didn't like Nikki; it was just that they never really thought much about him. He would always sit quietly at his desk, lost in his thoughts. Earlier in the year, Buster Billings and some of his buddies tried to tease Nikki because of the raggedy clothes and big floppy boots he wore to school every day. But Nikki would just sit there and stare out of the classroom window at the narrow pathway that led into the dense forest behind their school.

Pretty soon, Buster and his pals decided that teasing Nikki just wasn't worth the effort and finally left him alone. It wasn't too long before Miss Farley stopped calling on him in class. As the year went by, Nikki just sort of blended in with the desks, chairs, and tables in the classroom.

Each day after school was over, Nikki would gather up his books, quietly slip out of the classroom, slowly walk to the edge of schoolyard, and disappear into the lush woods that surrounded his school. Nestled deep within the tall trees, was a small cabin where he lived with his elderly grandmother.

Grandma Smith was a kind woman, but she rarely spoke to Nikki. She spent most of her days sitting quietly in an overstuffed, old armchair knitting sweaters, many with beautifully embroidered images of trees, leaves, and forest animals. Once every month, Nikki would carry the sweaters his grandma made to the General Store in Mill City where they were sold. Just about everyone in town had one of Grandma Smith's sweaters.

Nikki loved the woods. It was quiet there, and he felt safe among the towering trees with their gnarly roots that spread like tentacles under a soft layer of pine needles.

As he wandered through the woods around Grandma Smith's cabin, he would often think of his life before the fire, when his Mom and Dad were still alive. He could remember the long walks they took together in the vast green forest that surrounded their old house. But three years ago, the fire had taken his house, just as it had taken his beautiful forest, and worst of all, his Mom and Dad.

Nikki knew he could not replace his home or his parents, but he could help his precious forest begin to grow again. That is why for several years, he had been digging up small seedlings from the woods that surrounded his Grandmother's cabin and replanting them several miles away in the charred remains of the forest he loved as a child.

One evening just as the day surrenders to the night, Nikki was planting the last of his seedlings when he was overcome with an intense feeling that he was not alone. The daylight had faded, and a shadow gray evening mist settled upon the field. He felt a warm breeze sweep through the field of grass, and then heard what sounded like the wind whispering his name…"Nikki."

The tone of the whispering wind sounded strangely like the voice of his father. Before he could think much about it, he once again heard his name being whispered as a forest sparrow appeared through the mist and gracefully settled on the back of a stately twelve-point white-tailed buck. For a few fleeting moments, the sparrow and the deer stared back at Nikki before disappearing into the evening mist. Nikki closed his eyes as his heart once again felt the love of his parents.

Nikki's favorite time of day was when the sun is sinking low and the darkness of dusk spreads its velvet blanket over the forest. It is at this time that Nikki's real friends, the small animals of the forest, begin to appear. The animals had come to trust Nikki and would often follow him on his travels through the woods as he gathered his seedlings.

One evening, Nikki was resting quietly on an old tree stump when he heard a strange laughing sound echo through the trees. Nikki had heard just about every sound the woods could possibly make, but this was certainly not one of them. As he quickly stood up from where he was seated, Nikki once again heard the peculiar high-pitched laugh. This time it seemed to be getting a bit louder.

He quickly turned and, to his surprise, glimpsed a flash of something green disappear behind the base of a huge Ponderosa Pine tree. Holding his breath, Nikki slowly circled the tree. Nothing was there. Suddenly, a pine cone ricocheted off the side of his head and landed on the ground next to him. Startled, Nikki glanced up and saw a small elf-like creature no more than three feet tall perched on a tree branch staring back at him!

The strange looking creature had thick long brown hair and was clothed in a loosely fitting forest-green cape. On top of its head sat a pointed green cap. The most noticeable thing about this short little man was his pair of exceptionally large pointed ears. The rest of the creature's face was no less astonishing. Two oversized bright eyes set in a face the color of the forest seemed to glow a bright forest green, as the creature peered down at Nikki.

For what seemed like a long time, the two simply stared at each other. The woods was absolutely silent when to Nikki's surprise, the curious looking creature leapt from the branch where it was sitting and landed softly on the ground right in front of a startled Nikki.

Caught off guard, Nikki took two quick steps back, and in a frightened voice, asked, "What are you doing in my forest?" As the words left Nikki's mouth, the strange looking figure did a back flip and landed with his little legs spread wide apart and both hands planted firmly on its hips.

"Oh dear, please forgive me, Little Nikki, I didn't know this was your forest. Do you own it? When did you buy it?" he replied adding that same familiar high-pitched laugh.

Now totally confused, Nikki could think of little else to say except, "I'm sorry. I didn't mean it was mine. I just meant, well, I've never seen anyone here before, and you surprised me. Hey, wait a minute. How did you know my name?"

The little man smiled broadly, showing a mouth full of teeth that looked like wood chips, and replied, "Well Nikki, it's my job to know everything about these woods. I'm a Tree Keeper!"

"What did you say your name was? Tree Keeper?" Nikki asked.

"Heavens no!" the little creature responded. "My name is Bark, and I am a Tree Keeper. Just like your name is Nikki, and you are a boy. Got it?"

"Yea, I got it. Your name is Bark, but what in the world is a Tree Keeper?" the boy persisted.

"Good question," Bark replied. "A Tree Keeper is many things, but when you get right down to it, I'd say a Tree Keeper is a kind of caretaker."

"Okay, but what do you take care of?" questioned Nikki.

"Well, trees mostly, but other things that live in the forest, too. Like those little animals that follow you on your walks," Bark replied. "As a matter of fact, it was your little animal friends who convinced me that you mean no harm to my forest."

"You mean you talk to animals?" asked Nikki.

"Sure. Animals, trees, and even little boys, when I want to," Bark replied with a smile. "But for now, I'm on my way. I've got some trees that need tending. Enjoy your walk, Nikki, and I'm sure we shall meet again very soon." And with that, Bark gave another high-pitched laugh and was gone as quickly as he had appeared, leaving Nikki scratching his head in confusion.

Over the next several months, Bark often visited Nikki on his daily travels through the woods. They would talk long into the night. Nikki asked many questions about how to take care of the different kinds of trees growing in the forest. It quickly became perfectly clear that Bark knew everything about trees; how fast they grow, what they looked like when they were sick, how to make them better, and just about anything else anyone could possibly want to know.

After some time, the Tree Keeper began to teach Nikki the language of the forest which he called "Woodish". This beautiful and whimsical language sounded like the wind as it rustled through the woods. Bark taught Nikki how to use this strange but enchanting language to communicate with all the things that lived in the forest.

Bark was a cheerful little fellow; however occasionally, a deep sadness fell upon him when he would question Nikki about the "Big People" who lived outside his woods. Bark was concerned because so much of his beloved forest was being chopped down and taken away by them.

One evening, under a star-filled sky, Bark and Nikki were resting comfortably in the nook of a towering Chestnut Oak tree after a long and tiring hike. Bark smiled and said, "Nikki, you look a might bit thirsty."

"I am, Bark," the boy replied, "But I forgot to bring something to drink."

"Nikki, if you are going to live in the woods, you must always be prepared," Bark said with a twinkle in his eyes. He then reached under his cape and pulled out a small wooden cup and a well-worn leather pouch that looked as if it contained some sort of liquid. He proceeded to slowly pour a small amount of the thick, green liquid into the wooden cup. A smoky vapor poured over the edge of the cup, as an earthy aroma of moss and leaves filled the hollow.

Bark smiled broadly, handed the cup to Nikki, and whispered, "This should do the trick."

Nikki slowly raised the cup to his lips and began to sip the strange looking drink. Almost immediately, he felt a comforting warmth spread throughout his body. Nikki blinked several times as the forest around him seemed to glow bright green, and the damp, musty smell of earth and wood filled his senses. "Wow!" exclaimed Nikki, "What is this stuff?"

Bark laughed his high-pitched laugh and replied, "Just a little of my Tree Juice with bits of nuts, flowers, berries, and rainwater thrown in for good measure. How do you feel?"

"Kind of weird but okay, I guess," he answered.

"A little Tree Juice helps unlock the mysteries of the woods. Tree Keepers drink it often," Bark replied with an impish grin. "Now relax, take a bit of a rest, and dream the dreams of a Tree Keeper." And with that, Nikki quickly fell into a deep and peaceful sleep under a star filled sky. He dreamed of trees and leaves and the whispering wind.

Early the next morning, Nikki awoke amazingly refreshed on a comfortable bed of moss covered by a thick blanket of leaves. Bark was nowhere to be found. Not wanting to be late for school, he hurried home.

As he was combing his hair, Nikki noticed that it seemed slightly thicker and longer than usual, and his ears looked just a little bit larger than normal. When Nikki slipped on his shirt and pants, they seemed just a little too big, and he had to roll up his sleeves and pant legs.

Nikki arrived at school, walked to his desk, and sat down. To his surprise, his feet barely touched the floor, and his legs swung freely beneath his desk. Nikki thought this was rather odd, but he didn't give it a second thought, as his mind drifted back to the satisfying and restful night he had just spent with Bark in the woods.

Slowly, the leaves of the forest began to turn golden brown, and each morning a thin vale of frost covered the ground. The cold northern wind made its annual visit to the Montana woods. Soon, a soft layer of snow blanketed the forest, and winter silently settled upon the land.

Bark's home was hidden deep within the forest nestled away in the hollow of the ancient oak tree. Thin vines hung from its huge limbs, each containing a small sack filled with Tree Juice. Nikki and his forest friend continued to meet there often to speak of trees and other things of the woods. They were warmed by thick green Tree Juice sipped from wooden cups. Nikki was spending more and more time in the woods and less and less time in Mill City.

Nikki could sense that he was changing in many ways that winter. His understanding and appreciation of his beloved forest increased with every passing day spent with Bark. As his knowledge of the forest grew, so too did the length of his hair, and strangely enough…the size of his ears!

The days turned to weeks, and the weeks turned to months, until winter finally lost its frozen grip on the forest, and life once again began to return to the woods.

One warm spring evening, Nikki was on his way through the woods to meet Bark when he stopped for a moment and gazed up at the heavens. The silver moon cast a pale glow over the forest, and a thousand stars seemed to float in the silent night sky. He once again heard the wind softly whisper his name and then remembered the silhouette of the lone sparrow perched on the back of a white-tailed buck standing in the clearing at the edge of the woods. Nikki shut his eyes, and remembering the warmth of his parent's love, now understood that their spirit would live on forever in the forest they treasured.

Nikki walked to a clearing in the woods and sat down on the old tree stump where he had first met Bark many months ago. Bark was nowhere to be found. After several minutes, Nikki glanced to his right and noticed what looked like a small package covered with spindly twigs lying among the roots of an ancient oak tree.

The unusual package was wrapped in what looked to be light brown burlap. It was tied with long thin gray lengths of grass much like a ribbon that would be used to wrap a birthday gift. Nikki carefully untied the grass bow and then slowly began to open the mysterious package.

A broad smile appeared on Nikki's face as he gazed down at a small forest-green cape and pointed cap. He pulled the cap over his long brown hair until it rested snugly above his two extremely large pointed ears. Nikki gave out an extraordinarily high-pitched laugh, as he kicked off his floppy boots and slowly started to unbutton his shirt.

The next day, old Grandmother Smith called the Mill City Police Department to report that her grandson, Nikki, was missing. The sheriff searched the woods around Grandmother's cabin, but the only things he found were some old raggedy clothes and two big floppy boots.

As word quickly spread of Nikki Smith's disappearance, more and more of the townsfolk joined the search for the boy who walked in the woods. Even though he was never found, everyone seemed to believe that Nikki was still somewhere in the vast forest surrounding the town. In the weeks and months that followed, the people of Mill City, Montana often spoke fondly of the Smith boy and began to feel a new appreciation for the beauty of the forest and the importance of all the creatures that lived there.

Spring and summer came and went, and when school started that fall, Miss Farley and all the children in her class felt sad to see that Nikki's desk was empty. That year, they would often glance out of the classroom window hoping to catch a glimpse of the boy who loved to walk in the woods.

The following spring, something very special happened to the burned out forest surrounding the old Smith home where Nikki lived as a child. As if overnight, thousands upon thousands of small trees began to grow, and on what was once a charred and barren land, a magnificent, lush green forest appeared.

It is often said by the townsfolk of Mill City that, if you listen closely, you can sometimes hear a strange high-pitched laugh coming from the woods around the old Smith house… when the sun is sinking low and the darkness of dusk spreads its velvet blanket over the forest.

Geoff Collins

After retiring from a successful career in business, Geoff followed his passion for reading and writing by teaching elementary school. He resides in Charleston, South Carolina with his wife, Sally, and their children: Max, Leigh, and KC and his grandchildren, John and Collin.

Danner James

Danner James began his career as an artist with the Franklin Mint and has worked as a book illustrator and fine portrait artist for more than 30 years. Currently, Danner lives in the Greater Charleston area with his wife and daughter.

 # The Christmas Token 

⭐⭐⭐⭐⭐ "The Christmas Token is a heart-warming holiday tale about generosity, memories, and family."

⭐⭐⭐⭐⭐ "The artwork in this tender story is superior!"

⭐⭐⭐⭐⭐ "The Christmas Token should become a family tradition to read as the Christmas season begins!"

⭐⭐⭐⭐⭐ "Excellent!"

⭐⭐⭐⭐⭐ "Lovely book! My kids have read it many times over the holidays."

The Adventures of Archibald & Jockabeb

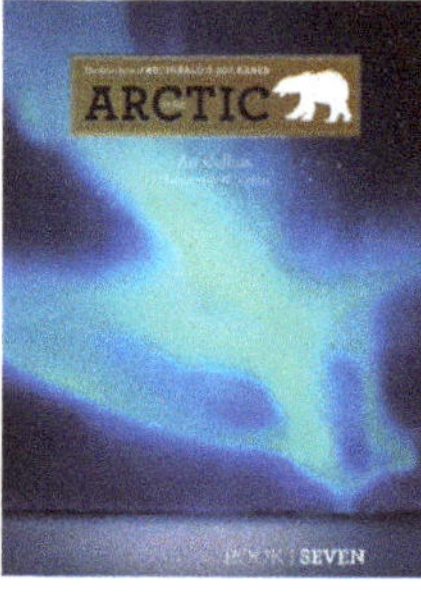

★★★★★ **"One of a Kind!"**
This is the best book EVER!!!!!! Dragons, Indians, horses, evil crows, there is nothing like it! I loved it…can't wait for more adventures to come.

★★★★★ **"A majestic tale - Harry Potter meets The Indian in the Cupboard"**
Loved reading this book. I quickly got hooked, dug in, and engaged with the characters. A wonderful story!

★★★★★ **"Rich in Vocabulary!"**
This book is rich in vocabulary. I can't wait to read all the other Archibald and Jockabeb books!

★★★★★ **"Best of the Best!"**
In the Forest is an outstanding book! The characters are great and help make the wonderful story come together.

★★★★★ **"Terrific series of action books!"**

Reading Partners is a nonprofit literacy organization that recruits and trains community volunteers to provide one-on-one reading tutoring to students in under-resourced schools across the country. This highly-effective program has helped thousands of children master the fundamental reading skills they need to succeed in school and beyond.
For more information, please visit
www.readingpartners.org

"Literacy is not a luxury; it is a right and a responsibility. If our world is to meet the challenges of the twenty-first century we must harness the energy and creativity of all our citizens."

-President Bill Clinton